LA LLORONA

Lah Jor-OH-nah

★ Famous Mexican Ghost. Her terrifying cry echoes through the night sending shivering children under the covers.

★ **Battle Cry:** *¡Ayyyyyy, mis hijos!*

★ **Lucha style:** Takes children away to make them her own

EL EXTRATERRESTRE

El Extra-teh-RES-treh

★ Space explorer, first reported hovering over the earth in his flying saucer in 1947.

★ **Secret desire:** To see the world

★ **Lucha style:** Abduction

MAROMAS VOLADORAS

MASCARA VS CABELLERA

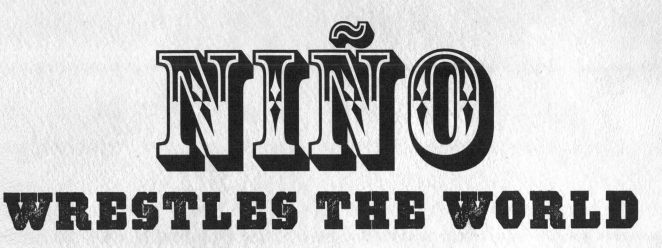

NIÑO
WRESTLES THE WORLD

YUYI MORALES

A NEAL PORTER BOOK
ROARING BROOK PRESS
NEW YORK

LUCHADORES

TÉCNICOS VS RUDOS

Niño!

SEÑORAS Y SEÑORES

Put your hands together for the fantastic, spectacular, one of a kind . . .

So superb are his talents that out-of-this-world contenders line up to challenge him.

Here comes the first one!

It is

THE
GUANAJUATO
MUMMY!

NIÑO
VS
LA MOMIA
DE GUANAJUATO

Oh, no!
What's a *niño* to do?

Niño defeats the Guanajuato Mummy
with the Tickle Tackle!

Uh-oh,

OLMEC HEAD awaits his chance
to bump skulls with Niño!

NIÑO
VS
CABEZA OLMECA

What will Niño do now?

Niño makes his Puzzle Muzzle move
and Olmec Head's mind is blown!
It is a real skull-cracker!

NIÑO
VS
LA LLORONA

Niño's Doll Decoy stuns the
WEEPING WOMAN
into submission!

NIÑO
VS
EL EXTRATERRESTRE

Marble Mash! Niño wins again!

. . . too terrifying for him.

Niño does it once more.
Look at the Popsicle Slick!

Tick-tock!

Tick-tock!

Tick-tock!

But then the dreadful hour arrives. Oh, no!

His sisters' nap is over. Time for Niño to tangle with

LAS HERMANITAS!

Las Hermanitas are *rudas*.

Way to hold!

What a move!

Niño's best move ever:

If you can't defeat them . . .

join them!

LOS TRES HERMANOS

now
accepting

ALL COMERS

¡VIVAN LAS

NOTES ABOUT LUCHA LIBRE

Lucha libre is a theatrical, action-packed style of professional wrestling that's popular throughout Mexico and many other Spanish-speaking countries. In lucha libre, wrestlers, called luchadores, wear bright, colorful masks that represent everything from animals to mythical figures to ancient heroes and villains. They wrestle individually or as tag teams and often perform against the backdrop of stories with elaborate, twisting plot lines. Like Niño, many luchadores wear masks to hide their identities, some even outside of the ring. El Santo, the most famous luchador in history, was buried in his mask, and his true identity was never revealed to his fans. During matches, luchadores often attempt to unmask their opponents as a way of asserting dominance.

LUCHAS!

Copyright © 2013 by Yuyi Morales

A Neal Porter Book

Published by Roaring Brook Press

Roaring Brook Press is a division of Holtzbrinck Publishing Holdings Limited Partnership

175 Fifth Avenue, New York, New York 10010

mackids.com

Library of Congress Cataloging-in-Publication Data

Morales, Yuyi.

Niño wrestles the world / Yuyi Morales. — 1st ed.

    p. cm.

"A Neal Porter Book."

  Summary: Lucha Libre champion Niño has no trouble fending off monstrous
opponents, but when his little sisters awaken from their naps, he is in
for a no-holds-barred wrestling match that will truly test his skills.

ISBN 978-1-59643-604-6 (hardcover)

[1. Wrestling—Fiction. 2. Monsters—Fiction. 3. Brothers and
sisters—Fiction. 4. Imagination—Fiction.] I. Title.

  PZ7.M7881927Nin 2013

  [E]—dc23

                2012012989

Roaring Brook Press books are available for special promotions and premiums. For details
contact: Director of Special Markets, Holtzbrinck Publishers.

First edition 2013

Printed in the United States of America by Worzalla,
Stevens Point, Wisconsin.

10 9 8 7 6 5 4 3 2

EL CHAMUCO

El Cha-MOO-koh

★ Powerful and rebellious, he likes to tempt people into doing bad deeds!
★ **Temperament:** Fiery
★ **Lucha style:** Placing obstacles and causing downfalls

LAS HERMANITAS

Las Er-mah-NEE-tahs

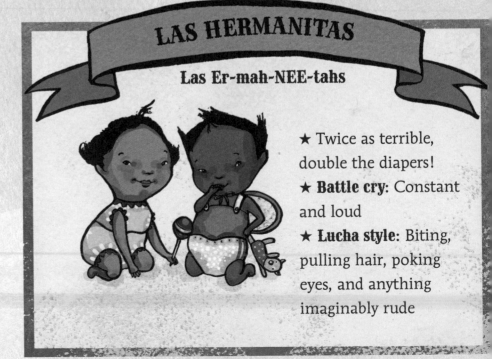

★ Twice as terrible, double the diapers!
★ **Battle cry:** Constant and loud
★ **Lucha style:** Biting, pulling hair, poking eyes, and anything imaginably rude